Illustrated by Tommy Stubbs

A GOLDEN BOOK · NEW YORK

Thomas the Tank Engine & Friends™

CREATED BY BRITT ALLCROFT

Based on The Railway Series by The Reverend W Awdry.
© 2008 Gullane (Thomas) LLC.
Thomas the Tank Engine & Friends and Thomas & Friends are trademarks of Gullane (Thomas) Limited.
Thomas the Tank Engine & Friends & Design is Reg. U.S. Pat. & Tm. Off.
HIT and the HIT Entertainment logo are trademarks of HIT Entertainment Limited.
All rights reserved. Published in the United States by Golden Books, an imprint of Random House Children's Books, a division
of Random House, Inc., 1745 Broadway, New York, NY 10019, and in Canada by Random House of Canada Limited, Toronto.
Golden Books, A Golden Book, and the G colophon are registered trademarks of Random House, Inc.
www.randomhouse.com/kids/thomas   www.thomasandfriends.com

Library of Congress Cataloging-in-Publication Data is available upon request

ISBN: 978-0-375-84382-2
PRINTED IN MALAYSIA   10 9 8 7 6 5 4 3 2 1   First Edition

It was a beautiful day on the Island of Sodor. Thomas was high in the hills, bringing some freight cars to the wharf. At an unfamiliar junction, he saw an old, overgrown track that looked like a shortcut.

Soon he was rattling down the steep track.

"No one has been down here for a very long time!" he huffed.

Then Thomas gasped. "Fizzling fireboxes!"

He had arrived at a station. It, too, was overgrown, rusty, and very old. There were crumbling platforms, and the station building was covered in ivy. Thomas had never seen such an amazing sight!

"What a funny place to have a station!" he peeped, and looked around some more.

"There are so many buildings. It looks like an old town!" he cried. "I cannot wait to tell everyone about this!"

So Thomas bumped and bashed along the old track and finally made his way down to the wharf.

The next day, the news of Thomas' discovery was all over Sodor. Sir Topham Hatt wanted to visit the hidden town at once.

"Thomas, you have made a wonderful discovery. This was the town of Great Waterton! When steam engines first came to Sodor," Sir Topham Hatt said, "this was an important town. It was called Great Waterton because the springs here provided water for everyone on the island."

"Why does no one live here now?" puffed Thomas.

"The springs ran dry, and the people left to live in new towns. The maps were lost. Everyone thought the town of Great Waterton was lost forever, too."

"But now it is found!" cheered Thomas.

"And if we work hard," added Sir Topham Hatt, "we can have the rededication of the town on Sodor Day!"

In no time, all of Sodor was working hard to fix up Great Waterton. Because Thomas had rediscovered the town, Sir Topham Hatt put him in charge of all the repair work. It was also Thomas' responsibility to explore all the old tracks around Great Waterton. Thomas liked checking old lines, and he liked being in charge. He wanted to show everyone he could do everything!

But one day there was trouble! Thomas was puffing too fast and the track was too old. He toppled off the track. Harvey came to lift him back on, but Thomas was bumped and bruised and had to go to the Works.

While Thomas was at the Works, a friendly new engine named Stanley was put in charge at Great Waterton. Every day, engines coming to the Works talked about how Really Useful Stanley was. Thomas started to feel a little jealous.

"*I* found Great Waterton," he puffed. "I'll be back! I'll be in charge again! And then everyone will see I'm more useful than Stanley!"

When Thomas was as good as new, he hurried back to
Great Waterton. A lot had changed.

"My! The tower and the junction both look as they must
have long ago!" cried Thomas. "Everything looks wonderful!"

Soon Thomas found Sir Topham Hatt—and Stanley was with him.

"Hello, Thomas!" chuffed Stanley.

Thomas peeped back . . . but very quietly.

"Stanley has done a good job. Work is moving fast," Sir Topham Hatt declared. "So I have decided that Stanley will stay in charge and you will help him."

Thomas' funnel flattened! He had lost the most important job of all.

The next day, Stanley asked Thomas to shunt some freight cars. Thomas was very good at shunting freight cars. And he also really liked doing it. But he didn't like Stanley telling him what to do.

Still, he wanted to show everyone how Really Useful he was, so he shunted freight cars all over Great Waterton. Then he remembered seeing an old freight car stuck in front of the old, abandoned Morgan's Mine. "I'll bring that last one in and Sir Topham Hatt will give me my old job back." Thomas smiled.

At last, Thomas found the old freight car, and he buffered up. But he biffed the car too hard. It rolled forward and disappeared into the mine!

"Cinders and ashes!" exclaimed Thomas. "Where did it go?"
Thomas moved ahead and peered inside.

"I must finish the job!" he huffed. "I'll soon find that freight
car." And Thomas puffed into the mine. . . .

It was very dark. Thomas was happy he had a bright lamp!
He looked ahead and saw the freight car rolling away down a
slope. Then it disappeared around a bend.

"Bust my buffers!" puffed Thomas. "I'd better go after it!"

Thomas whizzed down the steep slope. "Whee!" he whistled,
and "Whoaaa!" he cried. It was scary, but it was very exciting!
Thomas had almost caught up to the freight car.

"You won't get away from me!" he whistled happily.

But Thomas didn't notice the junction ahead! The freight car whizzed to the right. But Thomas sped to the left . . . and saw that the tunnel ahead was blocked!

"Oh, no!" cried Thomas, and he crashed straight through the blocked tunnel and jumped the track! Now Thomas was deep in the mine in a dark tunnel. To top it all off, his fire had gone out! His boiler would soon grow cold. And there was no one around to hear his whistle.

The next morning, Stanley and the other engines arrived for work.

"Where's Thomas?" Stanley asked.

The engines looked around—Thomas wasn't there.

Thomas was missing!

It was the biggest calamity Sodor had ever known!

Everyone looked for Thomas. They checked the quarries.

They searched
the docks.

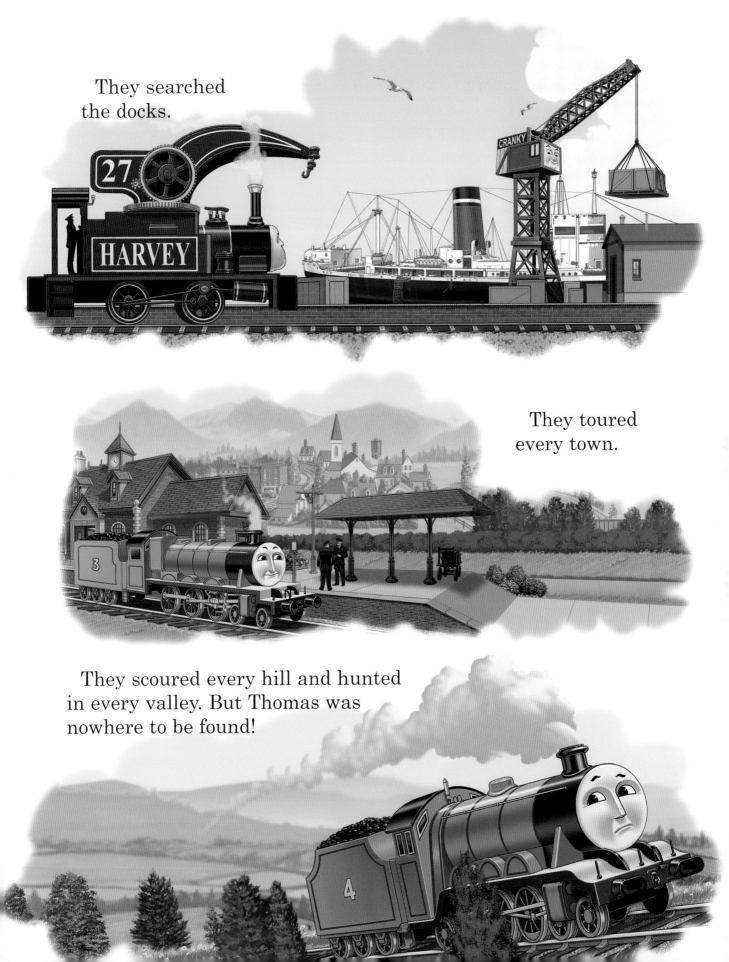

They toured
every town.

They scoured every hill and hunted
in every valley. But Thomas was
nowhere to be found!

And then Stanley had a thought. "Maybe Thomas is up on the forgotten tracks around Great Waterton. I'll look for him there."

When Stanley was high up in the hills, he whistled and whistled. "Where are you, Thomas?" But only his echo came back.

Stanley looked everywhere. Then he spotted Morgan's Mine. "Could Thomas have gone into the mine?" Stanley wondered. He whistled one last time . . . and this time, Thomas heard him.

"It's Stanley!" he gasped.

With his very last puff . . . and his very last huff . . .
Thomas blew his whistle as loudly as he could . . .

And Stanley heard him! He slowly entered the dark mine.
"Thomas!" he whistled happily. "Is that you?"

Thomas had run out of puff. He couldn't whistle again.
He could only wait and hope that Stanley would find him.

It wasn't long before Thomas heard Stanley chuffing up
behind him.

"Stanley!" he peeped. "I'm very happy that you are here!"

"Thomas!" whistled Stanley. "I'm very happy to find you. Where have you been?"

"I was trying to be a Really Useful engine," tooted Thomas.

"Don't worry, Thomas," Stanley chuffed. "I'll have you back on the track in no time!"

Soon Stanley was coupled up to Thomas. He pulled and tugged. Thomas was heavy, but Stanley didn't give up.

"I can do it!" Stanley wheeshed, and with a mighty heave, he pulled his friend back onto the track.

"Hooray!" tooted Thomas.

Then there was a very loud crack. The valve in Stanley's boiler had burst! Stanley was a strong engine . . . but pulling Thomas had been too much. Now Stanley couldn't move!

"Don't worry!" whistled Thomas. "It's my turn to help you! With your coal, I can push you home."

Stanley smiled.

In no time at all, Thomas' boiler was bubbling and his steam was wheeshing. Thomas found an open siding, got behind Stanley, and started to push.

"Here we go, Stanley!" Thomas huffed happily.

Stanley smiled back. And puff by puff, Thomas pushed Stanley up and out of the mine. The old tracks rattled and creaked, but Thomas didn't mind. He was happy and proud to push his new friend Stanley home.

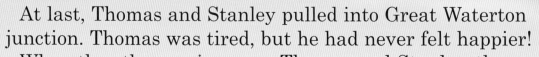

At last, Thomas and Stanley pulled into Great Waterton junction. Thomas was tired, but he had never felt happier!

When the other engines saw Thomas and Stanley, they tooted and whistled, and soon the sound of engine whistles echoed all around Great Waterton.

The news quickly spread throughout Sodor. "Thomas has been found!" the engines whistled.

Sir Topham Hatt grandly proclaimed, "Stanley saved Thomas, and Thomas saved Stanley!"

For the next couple of days, everyone worked hard to get Great Waterton ready for Sodor Day. Now Thomas was happy that Stanley had come to Sodor. Thomas had a wonderful new friend.

And just in time, everything was done.

The weather on Sodor Day was perfect! Sir Topham Hatt arrived and beamed, "Well done to you all! This is the grandest Sodor Day ever!" He and Lady Hatt stood beside the red ribbon with a great big pair of scissors.

"Thanks to Thomas, Great Waterton is no longer lost! And thanks to Stanley, the work was finished Right On Time. Welcome to the town of Great Waterton!" boomed Sir Topham Hatt.

Lady Hatt snipped the ribbon.

"We're all Really Useful Engines," puffed Thomas happily. He couldn't have been prouder!